To Sandy Rice

PRAISE FOR PATRICK O'LEARY

"Patrick O'Leary's new poetry collection, *Obviously I love you but if I were a bird*, sonnets and free verse, has all the strengths I came to love in his novels and stories — wonderful imagery, imagination, humor and depth."

— Jeffrey Ford, author of *AHAB'S RETURN*

"*Obviously I love you* begins with an auto-biography in sonnet form giving voice to existential questions as well as to intimately observed and felt moments of delight and grief. Outrage at injustice and tenderness for the vulnerable weave the sonnet sequence and the free verse into a coherent tapestry of human experience."

— ANCA VLASOPOLOS
AUTHOR OF *LATE PEARLESCENCE*

"In the pages of *Obviously I love you but if I were a bird*, we meet the many facets of Patrick O'Leary: proud patriarch, disappointed patriot, a man intent on relearning the stranger he meets in the mirror. Here is the sore tenderness of a poet at peak linguistic performance, contemplating his own mortality. Birth, divorce, children, devotion, books, memory, bitterness, beauty: his poems range abroad a spectrum of nuanced emotion and experience. O'Leary 'medicate[s] the darkness with [his] hope' and praises what lights it, while never neglecting to methodi-cally and acerbically examine the monsters crouching there, both without and within."

— C. S. E. Cooney
author of *SAINT DEATH'S DAUGHTER*

BOOKS BY PATRICK O'LEARY

OBVIOUSLY
I LOVE YOU
BUT IF I
WERE A
BIRD

OBVIOUSLY I LOVE YOU BUT IF I WERE A BIRD

PATRICK O'LEARY

FAIRWOOD PRESS
Bonney Lake, WA

Fairwood Press
21528 104th Street Ct E
Bonney Lake WA 98391

See all our titles at:
www.fairwoodpress.com

Cover image © George Peters / iStock
Cover and book design by Patrick Swenson

ISBN: 978-1-958880-37-1

Fairwood Press First Edition:
April 2025
Also available in ebook

Printed in the United States of America

Everyone takes a swing at the sonnet: Shakespeare, E.E.Cummings, John Berryman, Marilyn Hacker. The form is irresistible. A sonnet is character, monologue, imagery, philosophy, dance, seduction & revelation. It includes everything & excludes nothing. Infinitely adaptable, it permeates whatever story is imposed.

My first publication was a sequence of sonnets in India, *Indian Scholar Magazine*, 1980.

Sonnets became for me a comfort form, the last vestige of sanity in a vertigo world. At least we have rhyme. At least that makes sense.

Thanks to the editors & readers who liked these poems.

P.O. 5/2024

TABLE OF CONTENTS

SONNETS

FREE VERSE

SONNETS

"I know you will tell me I am a crazy old man to write sonnets—but since many people say that I have become gaga, I have to live up to my reputation."

—Michelangelo

Waiting for Michelangelo

The cozy sonnet is an assumption,
a homecoming which makes a poem welcome,
a bright frame to limit our perception
(to make it legible), a fine custom

which (when accepted & obeyed) spares us
the exhausting task of recreating
ourselves every second. The muse stares us
down on demand, but it thrives on waiting.

What it lacks in daring it quite provides
in discipline. What it loses alone
in novelty, neatness supplies. It hides
like a used skeleton asleep in stone

waiting for Michelangelo to break,
to carve a dinosaur & watch it wake!

Turtles all the way down

I stop for a small turtle in the road
to speed its deadly pilgrimage across.
It hisses as I lift it & I gog
& drop it. A very hostile hiss, Dude.

Triggering a memory of gore:
A cornered snapping turtle in a bog.
We teased it with sticks which bore
the marks left by his whip neck & sharp beak.

I pick up the turtle. We don't speak.
I take him to the other side. A cross
old woman yells at me, "Not there! The dog!"
Her happy poodle yapping at the door.

The road. The dog. The ditch. Dude, life is pain.
I can't look down at the turtle again.

Blessed are the etc.

God loves (a moving target, terrorists,
Limbo's worthy souls & scribblers on stalls,
Nagasaki, runaways who aren't missed,
my raped friend, my miscarried siblings,

a dozen unread Russian poets who
(His Son!) got electrodes pinned to their balls,
cowards & heroes coughing mustard gas,
stutterers, Nazis, Jews, junkies, Judas,

the photographers of Mt. St. Helens,
victims of unreported crime, dead stars,
the 50,000 senior citizens
in Detroit & their dependents who bring

home less than $5300*
a year, extinct birds, vivisections,) you.

*—1987

First snow

First snow. A flat grey light blares softly through
the windows. Make an angel? Fuck no. So
you smirk & watch the wet snow hurry fall
like Christmas traffic rushing to the mall.

(You're stuck.) But last night kids decorated
their gingerbread houses with elated
fierce devotion on the kitchen table
Every gumdrop, candy cane & wafer

placed reverently as host upon the tongue.
The cooked brown walls & roof became safer,
accrued the armor of the very young,
so sweet their concept of home: edible.

& the best part: There is no witch or stove
just the sweet dream of Santa & his love.

How love ends

Sometimes I watch my baby as he sleeps.
Sometimes before his open mouth I plant
two fingers, feeling for his breath. He keeps
breathing, but I keep making sure. I can't

forget the fact the radiator taught
him his first word! "Hot." I grow furious
& fret. Such revelations blunt & rot
my faith, but he grows sharp & curious.

The thing we wish most for the ones we love
is the one thing that can't be had—safety.
Yet it's not by drought, plague, wars, rumors of
wars, stupefying quakes of mystery—

But this child crying in the night whom, friends,
I cannot help—this. This is how love ends.

Morning moons

The moon is breaking into two round lumps
of dough in the blue sky behind the night
branches—lightning in reverse or curled
witch fingers holding up two balls of light.

An albino eclipse? The man has mumps?
The two-paned window must have a dual birth.
A single cell dividing. Come, my dear,
(Come see the end) before we disappear.

Calamity? I doubt you'll credit it
but there have been five extinctions on earth
since tender life—the single-cell—was hatched.
We survived. We'll survive this one, too. Watch.

Hold my hand. Look at that sky. Isn't it
a wonder anything holds in this world?

Necessary night

Behold: the magic of the Silver Screen
is based on the deception of the eye:
a third of every hour is spent between
the frames in utter darkness. Blank. But why?

We need our sleep: a third of our lives spent
in necessary night which frames the day;
we dream away the chaos & relent
our vision in relief. We wait & pray.

The word unsaid defines our ignorance,
creates the wound: the hole not the donut.
We read between the lines & we make sense
from silence; we deduct what God is not.

By process of elimination shown
the mystery that daily frames the known.

After Bergman's intro to the screenplay of *Wild Strawberries*

Self portrait

In an abandoned theatre late at night
I plotted once while playing hide'n-go-seek,
to break the rules & make a game of fright:
to terrify my friends & prove them weak.

So thrilling wild I dashed recklessly down
an empty corridor, flitted between
doors, tore back a curtain, sprang forth & found . . .
the darkest stranger I have ever seen.

I shrieked, jumped back; the hideous trickster
    mimed
as if he mocked my horror. I froze in fear;
the author of this evil shadow rhymed—
no stranger than my echo in a mirror.

I've seen my true intentions: terrible!
Your love alone has made them bearable.

Spam

My new friends--you overwhelm me. Elton
Cortes & Kaycee Priefert. Your concern
for my partner's pleasure & my private
stamina fills my mailbox & my heart.

You Mona Drummond & Leona Koch
are pioneers. You Purvis Brittany
& Preston Villalobos have put the
unmentionable back on the table.

Others may suspect your unlikely names
but I say Hail Enterprise! Hail Frazier
Matilda & Luella Champion,
Adolfo Marcum & Haley Tuttle!!

I hope you're paid fairly for your labor.
I just wish I could return the favor.

—Sorry, no rhymes

Temptation

The sonnet's temptation is to believe
that you are done once you have filled the form.
The hypocrite's devotion is so brief,
he punches in at church to chloroform

the cavity of conscience, parroting
goodness like a child reciting Shakespeare.
But art's not ours for the inheriting.
There are no guarantees—there's only fear

& trembling & the gift. For mystery
cannot be memorized. There's always doubt.
Faith's not obedience to gravity.
Beware the wonder of the word without

the flesh, the passion's pose without the loss,
the letter of the law without the cross.

The land without birds

There are no birds in that land, empty trees,
gutters, roofs. Buzzing clocks declare their dawn.
There are no wings convulsing on the breeze;
their streets are clean, their air is clear of song.

Their din was overruled & to insure against
a bad crop the Wise King conceived a scheme:
The populace was called to noise; commenced
A day of perfect racket, wail & scream.

The world below gone loud & mad & closed,
they mounted air, in terror they fell & died.
The land was speckled; all the streets were hosed.
A day's flight was their limit in the sky.

There are no birds there now to sing its joys:
the polished land of silence bought by noise.

The terrible gift

The child wailed, wanting to go in the car
yet dearly wanting to remain at home.
The monkey with his fist stuck in the jar
desired it all, could not settle for some.

It is so human that we take this as so mean:
the torment of the questions that dumbfound,
the common state of being in between,
the quest for flight, the need for solid ground.

To violate the borders of His land,
to occupy the truth, to trespass clear,
is it my fault I dare to understand?
I am not there as long as I am here.

It is our gift & punishment, I sense,
we must endure our choice's consequence.

Theology

Perhaps a Doctor Drama: open heart
surgery on a ruptured plot which sans
continuity (scenes shot weeks apart
harnessed by violence together) (fans

don't care) requires pinpoint splicing to bring
the separate dangling strands to order
(a meat grinder in reverse). Quivering
stitched organs getting fat & saved under

the virtuoso needlepoint of these
rubber hands. The baffled audience lets
out a gasp. Applause. Bravo! Now it breathes—
it must be alive! It fits the sprockets—

it must be a movie! It has a thread
of plot—it's art! It must be food—it's dead!

Two stray leaves

Two stray leaves are all that's left in the black
delta of the bare red maple, hanging
like soggy moths, their wings folded & slack.
They've overstayed their welcome & clinging

to the family tree, separated
by years of branches, decades of distance,
they might as well be strangers. Related?
I wonder if they know the other's there.

Yet they share this foggy dawn, this aching
wind & a damp courage as they quake,
like dancers in the wings poised & waiting
for their final cue, when they'll leap & wake

& embrace the bright lights, answer the call
to spin, to fly, &, finally, to fall.

What is like

a babe's first word, an iceberg: most of it
is unknowable, a silent movie:
—stuck with a 3D joke—a 2D wit,
Pre-Newton Gravity, a lens: empty,

swelling the atom, shrinking the cosmos,
destroying distance, arriving nowhere,
gambler: only good in fits, shadows:
the shape of something blocking light, a mirror,

safety: between the stirrup & the ground,
the vivid haunting of an absent limb,
senility: the fury & the sound???
Give up. It is a riddle told to dim

fools who pass it on to children dreaming
who wake into a sleep & forgetting.

We agree

The New Year. One more sunrise. One less wife.
We share a home we lost our love in. Huddle
one last time. Scared. Sad. Old friends comfortable
in our closeness & departure. Why bother

fixing it? We're not broke—It is. Our lives
can start. We're free, unstuck, redundant
Off-duty. We no longer have to fight
those old wars. No more struggle. We're both right.

Just not right for each other. We've agreed
to split our assets/debts down the middle.
There will be time to spar over where & how
& who gets the good china. Not now. Now

we feel the concussion of agreement.
At last! We agree! We've lost each other.

I officially prefer to forgo

I will now forgo the inconvenience,
The endless mindless bureaucratic shit
that keeps your motor humming—It makes no
    sense.
I forgo. Unsubscribe. Opt out. Get it?

I truly regret I was ever yoked
to your list & your org, I want off.
I dearly wish my membership revoked.
I merely want to reclaim all my time,

my privacy, my dignity, my mind
forever occupied in filling forms.
When did all this ever become the norm?
No more. I am off-duty. I am resigned.

I've stepped out of line. I'm here for the fun.
I forgo it. It's forgotten. I'm done.

FUNK (or American Radio sleeps on its feet)

Whilst fiddlers fidd(& wink)le bombardiers
take aim & beat about the Mystery Dance—
CRANK UP THAT JAM YOU VOODOO
      PIONEERS!
—Wake up! We have a party in our pants!

I've seen the Mother Lode, the open grave!
Once mute & glorious molten rock ERUPTS
& petrifies the bigots who are slaves
& slips the discs of wardens who are nuts.

Throw down your arms! Surrender to the groove!
(O Wild & Lava Hot Hipiphany!)
We're on the downside of this hill so S-L-I-D-E.
(Rome burns!) Abandon hate & cool all ye

who enter the vocabulary of
(Funk is real! (Alleluia!) God is) LOVE.

"The young writer . . . will hear the beat of new vocabularies, the exciting rhythms of special segments of his society, each speaking a language of its own. All of us come under the spell of these unsettling drums; the problem for the beginner is to listen to them, learn the words, feel the vibrations, & not to be carried away."

E.B. White, *The Elements of Style*, William Strunk Jr. & E.B. White, 2nd ed. (New York: Macmillan, 1972), p.81.

Beloved mom. My first abuser. Not

Beloved mom. My first abuser. Not
my last. I think I never recovered
from that first betrayal. The memory rot
remains. The miracle that I still loved.

"Just wait 'til you have kids," you used to frown.
Ruefully I discovered that you knew
parenting's tough. That day you threw me down—
I bet that was a tough day, too.

You left me needing so much, Beloved,
I trusted anyone. They rolled you out
in a blue bag, said I could leave the room.
Your last passage from the fire to the tomb.

"It's OK" I said. "That's not mom." You see
the moment you died was when you left me.

Oh carbuncle on the body politic—
My lance! My lance!

Oh spew, you empty golden bile spittoon.
Master of the multitudes of lying,
The man no-one-can-say-no-to cartoon.
In the end it all comes down to grabbing.

Is it too much to ask entry before
entrance? The simplest restraint for a boy
who knew none, a toxic whiny bore,
a total lack of character & joy.

Surely we'll wake up this November
& stop a spoiled dangerous man bereft
of honor, prowess, good. Remember:
a brat who doesn't know assault is theft.

Can't take it back. You can't be unviolated.
We are the long sought justice you've awaited.

Expecting

They do not tell you to expect torture.
just "contractions" "labor" delivery"
but python wrenched & wracked & drenched
so crammed in now that she forgot all why

for sixteen solid hours & razor four
I watch the one I love in agony.
I cope by fractions. Taut & spent by gore
a grunt a rip a push & it was (free!)

Ours . . . astounding . . . purple . . . slippery . . .
    boy . . .
so crammed in yes that we forgot all now
They cannot tell how to expect this joy.
There are no words. We hum. They stitch (O wow)

& when the acid hits your eyes you squeal
& then they jab the needle in your heel.

Truth in Stereo

As if someone had hollowed out my bones
& suddenly I found that I could fly:
upon our baby's ears I put headphones
& briefly stunned by (quicker than the ear)

the ghostly source that floated in his brain.
He strained his eyes to peer over his brow
then pulled them off to see & make it plain.
One here. One here. Nothing between. But how?

His raw mind worked its first arithmetic
& failing facts discovered mystery:
to get you here we played a little trick,
the magic of the hidden harmony.

A third is sung by merging of the two.
That music there—that's you my son—that's you.

The cities below me are rivers of light

In this season of the light returning
our gifts are everywhere like those stars there.
We know wherever you are, you're burning
& you shine. Little lights everywhere.

My lovely children are the constant goods,
the lights around my Christmas tree.
My funny youngest actor in the woods
builds houses on the grey & churning sea.

My first son talks fluent computer &
raises two blossoms of joy so sweet & bright.
My eldest talks to the deaf with her hands.
She too excels in the language of light.

Do not forget your light, your heart, your head.
Love yourself & be careful who you wed.

1957 Christmas morning

I wake on the couch to a tree laden
with lights that burn my eyes. Fever
Fever scorches my skin, my throat swollen
& cankered. I do not open my gifts.

I'm transported to hell: A hospital.
Everything is white hot especially
strangers who will not let me sleep, but feed
me needles wherever there is muscle.

My blood trickles down a straw. My star:
A candy striper reads me comics tells
me stories. I love you wherever you are.
Dad stashes orange popsicles on the sill.

I make a promise to the nearest god:
I'll never lie if you spare me the rod.

When everything I see makes no sense not

When everything I see makes no sense not
one word, not one thought, not a goddamn thing:
a tidal wave of bullshit & slow rot.
This old flat earth needs a rug cleaning.

It would be much too much without my wife.
I can't get through the day without caffeine
& her. Oh Light, she cracks me up. My life
began when I found I could made her laugh.

Her art is full of faces black & old
as seasons put their memories on wood
she scratches on the aging rings of fold,
etching out their histories with her blood.

Every sliver as prayerful as a monk
frozen fingers scribing Song of Songs drunk.

Dear silent zoologist—I'll go first

We're your favorite experiment: No doubt
that's why you trouble our skies with your lights
& creep into our nightmares, probe our nights:
you cannot wait to see how we turn out.

But, neighbor, do allow me one request.
We are not your toys. We are not your pets.
Please don't play with us. Really, at our best
we can learn much from each other, so let's.

We're good company, easy on the ear
& known to get companionable around
a smoke, a dog, a laugh, a view, a beer.
When all else fails we'll even be the clown.

Oh you who need nothing what are we good
for? Bait? Curiosity? Friendship? Food?

You shed all meaning like an old old coat

A long long journey that begins in doubt.
Ditch hell, drop incense, lose celibacy.
Too tight, too tattered, musty, out of style.
Just the facts please lose the mystery.

I sat my Mom down on my green bedside.
"I need the truth mom," I said with a gulp
& she explained life to me then. She lied.
"Santa brings most of the presents. We help."

You leave your faith by realizing how
it's not the dog that wags it is the tail.
Leave sin. Leave sacrifice. Leave prayer (& god).
That wasn't a garden; it was a jail.

Time's never been an easy path no doubt;
by the time you get to you, you're all out.

Sir, all your parts are out of warranty & that coupon is from the Sixties

When I turned 71 I woke late (Hell
Yeah) had great coffee & a bagel,
a bookstore (rare) as empty as a bell.
Two white girls read back to back agiggle

living bookends united in the aisle.
Infused joints to launch my new year over
& jettison my previous stages & guile
& watch them tumbling to earth. Sober.

25 years. Torched the middle ages.
I medicate the darkness with my hope,
scratching my useless words to fill pages.
A good beat, Effexor, my grandkids, dope.

You. For a time between the sky & earth
a shaggy old man got his money's worth.

The vine knows the root

I hold my grandson in arthritic hands.
He grabs my collar tightly red like rust.
That's a good instinct, Boy. But is it love?
I mean, what can a baby know of trust?

But when he smiles I swear, he understands
our bond goes deeper than this strange old dude.
I've passed my inspection. This blood knows blood.
I knew first time I talked to my daughter

on the phone I recognized her laughter.
It rang bawdy & unashamed & loud.
I knew we were family when she drove:
I stole a stare at her Irish face: proud,

flat & freckled & bonny fair mirrors
her mother whom I hadn't seen in years.

— *for Eli*

2024, stoned, listening to Dick Clark, heating pad

toasting my tippy sinking body: wince
is my brand, arthritic shoulder missing bursa
spider webs of pain my every clinch,
my oh so less than sprightly knees get worse,

my torn hip, herniated spine the rat
gnawing my right thigh, the odd broken tooth,
clouding vision, galaxies of dust that
smear my every sight, sleep apnea, truth?

Memories failing at the proper names,
deaf to dialogue, my Piston's saga,
addicted to subtitles, do I blame
PTSD, Anxiety, Maga?

I'm not the only one who's stuck, hero.
I toke & I don't give a fuck. Zero.

The chins & wattles appear like medals on old uniforms, waiting to be relieved

I grow my wattle at the speed of age.
I really only notice when it's done,
a new sag here, a new quite wrinkled page.
Fact is, it happens on its own & one

day I used to have eyelids, now I got
pouches, with blue jewels that lie & spark.
One day you're shaving the face of some not-
you, someone you've never met before. Dark

hairs in my nose, my swelling ears, body
bloats & melts into my latest disguise.
As I lose to gravity, my hobby
is sitting, moaning & playing at wise.

I say this to the young because it's true.
Thank god this will never happen to you.

We float, we lie, we sit, we crawl, we walk, we lie down

Death. Daunting though my waning days crack
on a rogue nerve waiting to be pinched, a pain,
an edifice rehearsing crumble, creak
we drag ourselves until we crawl on

like black slaves grinding up the pyramids
Fucked my shoulder loading firewood stacks.*
Arthritis. Pinched nerve in my back.
Once you start falling, you don't fall back

Funny, we start getting our hands & legs,
scramble to our feet as fast as as we can,
only to end up sitting, unable to stand, legs
aching every step, a shrinking old man

in bed unable to sleep, lost in a wilderness.
May it come before I forget my children. Yes?

*Possibly changing a tire on I-75

AI YI YI YI YI

Capitalism is the mindless tool
intent on making us invisible.
It wants only customers. If we buy
they don't care what we want or even why.

As long as profit rolls in the machine
rolls on & over anyone who lost.
But do we step away, cash out & glean
our stash? No!! That's the invisible cost!

We hoard our treasure till it buries us.
(I interrupt this sonnet just to say
A blind man could run this world better than this
dumb crap. There's got to be a better way.)

The richest men in the world have no idea how
to spend their treasure. They are lost in now.

There came upon him hard a time of grey

His ascent, it's true, had more or less peaked.
He had none of the dreams that haunted youth
(nor cash) but, all in all, his sins have passed
the only mercy time grants us is that

we get too tired to care & we forget.
Sins too many to count & too boring, too.
Yet not on soggy failures do I brood;
it is my successes. So hard earned. So

so useless. When every lost angel is
a remix, tribute, or satire. I'm sick.
Duran Duran & Monkees sell their piss.
It's Vegas, Disney, or Miami. Pick.

When all anyone wants is a good time.
Will knew. A laugh. A cry. A dog. A rhyme.

Tell me more about the Darkness staring back

I backed our car over our black cat Joe
took him to the vet then arrived late at
the funeral. Here's all I want to know:
Why the need for beasties who attack?

We're so hooked on the rush when lions miss.
Our spiffy golden never caught a squirrel
until he did. He gaped his jaws in bliss;
his prey escaped into the wilder world.

I've ditched the old sickening meme of hell
(so clearly a projection of our growl)
the old monsters can no longer compel
when calving icebergs make the blue sea howl

We hunt from meal to meal. Call ourselves god.
What then? The hunted forget they are food.

There is a madness about, a turning

There is a madness about, a turning,
a fever loose upon the broken land.
A toddler tantrum. The ever-banging
drum of Mine. Citizens! What can stand

against a country determined to self
-harm? You totter on a crumbling coast;
a fat palatial delusion of wealth—
entropy. Sitting on your stack. The most

successful hoarders on the good green earth.
But nobody laughs at your miserable junk:
The stuffed owner class who gild their worth,
whose biggest crimes are invisible gunk.

The hoard who want to be ruled & obeyed;
their minds surrendered to the holy blade.

Black Jesus 1967

My bus ride to school was a battle zone.
Whole blocks were missing teeth. Quiet piles of
Rubble. Gutted stores. Abandoned,
Detroit still smoldered from the riot.

Dad leaned his deer rifle against the door.
I rode past The Blind Pig on 12th (Cool)
(Tread marks of tanks on Rosa Parks Blvd.)
White boy going to inner city school.

Locals painted the white Jesus on the
corner black: his face & outstretched hands
Black. Somebody came & "corrected" it:
Back to white. The next day we painted it black again.

Detroit rebuilt. The Lions roar away.
& there black Jesus proudly stands today.

Three numbers

A naked man stands at his locker. Oh
no. Has he forgotten? Has he forgot?
Has he forgotten everything he knows
or is this just the very first forgot?

He stands dripping in his own puddle, then
locker doors are slammed by naked men.
He grips the combo dial; he tries once more.
Then tries the numbers that he tried before.

The black dial makes a reassuring purr.
The old world still wobbles on its axis;
wars wage, hearts break, kids fall, death & taxes.
Click, Click. The kindest sound a soul can hear.

The holy three numbers that will allow
him to escape this long terrible now.

Uncruel

We must undo the knot, uncruel the cruel,
One stitch, one code, one flaw, one law, one
    thought.
Expose the holy scams that keep us fools;
we must undo the cruel cruel world they've
    wrought.

Undo the needless deaths, get off the cross,
uproot the buried gold, unbind the bound.
Dig out the rotten core, burn off the dross.
Fix your northern star on what can be found.

Let others sleepwalk though this land of lies,
yoked to the rituals of blood which only gain
mercy from the silent gods who must despise
every unanswered prayer for every pain.

Choose hope though it is clearly clearly night.
We must uncruel the cruel cruel world with light.

Babel

They built a winding tower to God in Babel
to hear more clearly His voice, to quench
the many thirsts of all the rabble.
They built a corkscrew, then they got a drench

of noise. They heard no voice despite their labors.
They learned the skills they needed to ascend.
The knowledge of good & strange neighbors
who taught new ways with stone & cut & bend

who shared the most unusual meals & sang
the most unusual songs & though they rang
with words nobody understood the sound
you couldn't help but sing along. So man

so shocked his God when all the strangers sung,
He stopped. Because he knew His work was done.

The first person I saw die was on TikTok

The lovely lost eyes of the shot woman
looking at the iPhone filming her (gulp)
I watch awareness settle in her eyes.
Why the fuck are you shooting me? she seems

to say. Why aren't you going for help?
Can't you see I'm shot? Or is this a dream?
Then terror settles in her face, blood streams
from her mouth & nose. Death is a fact

& she is beautifully dead. What world?
What justice was worth this awful act!?
What god, tradition, custom, law or lies
were worth the loss of this lovely girl

who we will never know? What can be done?
The worlds we lose when we lose anyone.

Camouflage

Though we are not strangers to espionage,
perhaps we have underestimated the fact
the disappearing act of camouflage.
How pliable this rare self we hack.

Beats outrunning a beast: masquerade.
subterfuge & disguise. Chief tactic of survival:
invisibility. Why not hide? Chances of revival
are slim. The chances of you losing yourself fade.

There's no resisting who you are about.
Hide as you will you're bound to come up you.
Eventually you will wear yourself out.
It takes so much less effort to be you.

We're in the dark until we hatch human
we trust someone will come to catch us then.

The melt begins

The melt begins. The drifts dissolve downtown,
revealing litter on the soggy ground.
In Detroit it's hard to believe in spring.
So many have been left out in the gloom.

We enter the season of mufflers, rust
& moves. I call the number on the lawn.
Her son says she's in Assisted Living.
Did she fall? Forget his name? Burn the stew?

Did all the promise of her life come due?
Somebody left the old fat organ on,
presiding over the only lit room
in this silent interrupted home of dust.

A showy fantail of pedals, stops, keys,
lacking only feet, fingers & partner.

Dreams do not prepare us for the day

Bootcamp? Drills. Awful food. & loneliness?
The Dreaming is quite often just as stressed
as any day it hopes to be rehearsal for.
True terror invasive inescapable is here

& yet on waking we arise like gods
unmindful of the threats that loom as near
as our brain pan. Daughters, sons & bods
are we doomed like dreams to panics we cannot

escape & wake when waking is so sharp
& saddening? I've heard the theory that dreams
are mind maintenance, exhausting excess,
codifying the useful. Who can say

how memories do business. Dreams may play.
But dreams do not prepare us for the day.

Abedding Emily I shrank in terror

My first mistake was falling for those eyes.
I think I fixated on her black broach.
I couldn't take the silence & the chill,
I couldn't get a pause in edgewise.

She had her muse, her garden. Until
I passed her mossy gate & saw her coach
the dark horse at the green lane where I trod.
Paused. Black glove parted velvet curtains back.

She offered a ride downtown & I consented
Fine as any flower her modest scent.
Inside she pinned me to the couch,
we crossed the Rubicon & I was god.

I watched her sleeping; the night came & went.
Her first words when she woke: "You're kind
   & bent."

To the 75 million morons who voted for him

He'd take your money. Call you names & pinch
the girls. The meanest kid on the playground. .
But did you try to stop this painted Grinch?
You hoped he wouldn't notice you around;

everyone he noticed paid for it. He
acted like we were all in on the joke.
His misbehavior was his privilege, see?
Nobody stopped him. All his wealth was smoke.

You let him do it. He did it all. To
whomever. All you had to do to win
was laugh at his victims, too. You were in.
(At least now he wasn't picking on you.)

You let him take 666
kids from their parents. Yet you don't feel sick?

The blood, the race, the need, the thrall

Oh sweet oblivion suspended in
desire; the wave of now, the ache & glance
stokes hard the unbearable surge. Bare skin.
The catch of breath when flooded with the dance

of body kindness, laughter, hunger, grace
the dip & curl of muscle skin & bones,
the likable freckle on sated face
the cloud of scent, the barely muffled moans

the drum of the rump, the rows of toes, the odd
flaws that map our epidermis, Oh seed,
the curve of lip, the breath of wanting God
to merge, devour, complete the dance of need.

I perpetuate & I'm not alone.
I am not alone. We are not alone.

FREE VERSE

We are a forest full of trees

We are a forest full of trees
our roots go deep as history
we carry all our memories
We are a forest full of trees

We are a forest full of trees
We share the shade
We share the breeze
we share the rain
we share the sun
there is enough for everyone

We are a forest full of trees
We'll be here when the others leave
We've seen things that you can't believe
We seize the light
We cool the night
We never tell our mystery
We are a forest full of trees

Brahms Requiem

In the stunning suburban church
the orchestra delivers the goods
The choir swoons
The soloists soar
& the whole beautiful thing
goes on & on
But all the time they're playing
my eyes keep sliding over
to the stained-glass window
where the yellow-haired angel
is staying the hand of Abraham
The angel's hair curls upward in an S
& his wings are red
Abraham is surprised
He was all geared up for this
& Isaac his son is looking down & away
clearly traumatized
as his bare white torso & legs
are bound by red rope
& you want to stand up
in the middle of the church

walk over & reach into the window
& tell him: It's cool It's cool kid
This is just a lesson your dad had to learn
about faith & obedience
 See? He's putting away the knife
The angel came in the nick of time
God was just kidding! Isn't that great!?
It was just a test! A stupid stupid test
& your dad passed
& as you cut him free you realize
there's not enough room
on this window to tell the whole story
How Isaac will never be able to trust his father
    again
How Abe will never be able to meet his son's eyes
How the town will talk about the man
who took a blade to his own son's neck
& meanwhile the choir & the orchestra
& the soloists are going on & on about
how when the trumpet sounds
every faithful servant will be spared
Death where is thy sting?
Hell where is thy victory?
& in my mind one finger on my left hand rises
& points at one of the most horrific stories
in a book full of them & my mind says
There
It's right there

Up North

One day my dad had had enough
& he started packing
He packed his rods his tackle box & lures
his cooler a carton of Stroh's
the transistor radio
so he wouldn't miss the Tigers
He spent a long time packing
(He always was a neat man)
but he had to know
he could pick up
whatever he needed
on the way up north
(that's where he was heading)
Up North
That peculiar retreat Michiganders call
pretty much anywhere north of the thumb
A remote place of evergreens sand dunes
miles of beaches & curling silver rivers
teeming with rainbow trout
A man who has had enough
could find a welcome there
a place to sit & crack a can
cast his line & see what the current gave up

Now when he was packed
He told my mom
& she said fine
& he looked at her
(I can just see his face
proud defiant & wounded
all at the same time
—the worst poker face you ever saw)
So she said Fine you go
Have yourself a time
& leave me with these 5 kids
& I'll tell everybody what you did
I'll call your daddy your sisters your brothers
     & your boss
& let's see what they think about it
Well he didn't go
& she didn't tell anybody
except me some 25 years later
Who knows
Maybe she saw something familiar
in my face
That look men get when they have had it
when they are thinking about
packing everything they need
leaving everything they don't
& heading

Up North

Flight over Hollywood

It happened on one of those crazy roads
that snake up the Hollywood Hills
where James Dean had his knife fight
at the Griffith Observatory
We parked at a scenic overlook
to watch the sun dive into the ocean
like a perfect hillside pool
& this tanned body builder in a tank top
had a Styrofoam airplane
with wings about this wide
He launched it up into a vortex only he could feel
& the space fell away
as it rose above the valley
then somehow looped back
He must have plotted
its course to perfection
for it curved home on invisible currents
& he snatched it effortlessly
That would have been enough
but as we moved in to admire his craft
he slid back the transparent canopy

& showed us the pilot:
a tiny white mouse with pink claws & red eyes
& all the way to the bottom
down the steep & deadly roads
that skim the edges
of those crazy hills
I wondered about that mouse
What was the flight for him?
Sheer terror
or sweet transcendence?
Or something only small things can grasp
when they are loved & kept & freed
by crazy gods
& flung into the sky

I Knew

It wasn't the day I saw myself
in a newspaper ad I never posed for:
my simple smile, my name
stenciled on a pair of boy's mittens.
It wasn't the day I passed myself
on Woodward Avenue: while riding
a 10-speed, while driving a green VW bug:
you wouldn't believe the look on my faces!
It was the day I found myself
in a stainless steel room of masked
men & women: the day this lovely purple
boy ripped out of her body tugging
a yellow coiled balloon like you get
at the circus, his buddha's face
agog at too much light. This was the day
reality turned to gossip & mystery
got real & I knew I knew nothing.

David Mamet on Donuts

The thing is
The thing about donuts is
You can't eat the middle
The middle ain't there
It's a hole
& you can't eat holes
But try eating a donut
without the hole
You can't do it
That's a muffin Charlie
Real donuts are round
& they throw in a hole
but you can't eat it
That's the thing

Keep Looking

My neighbor rarely ventures out
Sometimes I see her
stepping down the drive
to get the paper
Always bundled
always timid
as if the task involved
some dare not evident to anyone but her

But this morning something stops her
on the usual path
& she pauses stunned
to see what spring
has done to the world
The sky a perfect slap of blue
The trees a riot of color
The smells tidal as a crowd cheering

& I find myself joining them
rooting for her stillness her
routine crumbling & look now

she covers her eyes with one hand
to look up at the birds
take it all in & you'd swear
she was saluting
before she retreats
& I'm practically out of my seat
doing a one-man wave whispering
Oh please keep looking
Don't stop now
Keep looking

The Interview

went well
Nobody mentioned my nakedness
The gaps in my resume
were presumed to be
exotic off-the-record intervals
which took me on missions
of International Import
to countries without hygiene
I did not discourage this biography
& if I hinted at midnight exchanges
of currency for hostages,
jungle rendezvous,
& camouflage makeup
—all the better
I felt no compunction to candor
For truly what resume
what history for that matter
encompasses
the human soul
& haven't we all felt
that given the crisis & the call
we would plumb vast reserves
of inner character

to do any great task
no matter the risk
It's just that well
there is so much on our plate

At this the interviewer nodded
& for the briefest moment
I saw that she too was naked
every one of her employees
every customer in the store
in fact the whole damn mall
had become a nudist colony
It took all my composure
to muster a final confession
& sigh as I said: Honestly
as much as we'd rather
it weren't true
the immediate concerns
of quota & deadline
cat food & condo
do not allow much occasion
for our heroic impulses
This last admission especially
impressed my new boss
And I think may have
won me
the job

The Transformation of Matter

I am what I ate

I am the ditch water I drank
in Bridgeport Michigan
that gave me trench mouth
on Christmas Eve
& put me in the hospital
when I was 5

I am forty years of iced tea
sitting on a deck
sipping down summer
watching the leaves
drink the sun

I am the hundreds of
Tanqueray dry martinis on the rocks
that soothed my gut
& rotted my soul

I am the clouds of Salem Lights
I inhaled for thirty years

I am Mom's Hungry Boy Casserole & Sloppy Joes
I am also the gaps between meals
that polite poetry does not mention
the long days of hunger
when I had no money

I contain multitudes
The quick banana
The pop tart
gallons of coffee
tubs of French fries
Every meal a memory
Every bite a redefinition of me

& from the outside
nothing happened at all
Patrick proceeded meal to meal
like a pinball
dinged between diners
while churning inside
was need & loss
appetite & picnic
transubstantiation
where the holy wafer
adopted the human body
as its home & fed the blood
that is our common fuel

& while all this god magic
was being performed
on a darkened stage
I stole the spotlight
& pretended to be the show
to take bows
for jokes that occurred to
carrots
& poems that sprung ripe
from apricots
& pledges of desire
that erupted from clams
& the grand plans & promises
that rose like mathematics
& Mozart
from the matter of lima beans

Radio

Hot summer nights
in the thick close air
on the front porch
Dad listening to
the Tiger Game
after a full day
on the railroad job
his Tareyton glowing
in the dark
orange & off
like a firefly
flirting with Ernie Harwell
as he ran down
the play by play
Sometimes
he'd let me
take the transistor upstairs
to my bedside
& huddle by
the green glow
my head pulsing

all night as
the world split open
like the birthing place
of a woman
& I was born again
in the dark
to the beat
to the miracles
they never sang about in church
or talked about downstairs
& nobody knew
that little boy
burst open
on those nights
& was made new
by heavy music
with skin
& blood
& wild desire
that played my body
& sent a night train
choogaloogin
down my spine
& Momma
once I caught it
I never got off

The Numbers

The wasted cityscape below
has more abandoned homes
than any budget
could afford to tear down
So they rest there
the way we all do eventually
empty of everything
but memories
The calamity has trickled 12 stories up
to the high-rise copper tower
with all the empty offices
Gleaming smiles with missing teeth
The lawyer has no admin
just an outer room where
we set our coats on chairs
It looks like people have melted
leaving only their outerwear
Behind a sparse desk he sits
& explains the concept of bankruptcy
It is important that we grasp
the numbers
the difference between

Chapter 7 & Chapter 13
I don't understand
He explains again
I still don't understand
& he gets mad
You're not listening he snaps
I give him 3 pieces of paper
my expenses
my assets
my debts
You're missing a piece of paper he says
Your income
I have no income I say
He smiles & says
O yes you do
I haven't had a job in 13 months
You have a pension & unemployment?
Yes
It takes half my pension
to cover my family's healthcare
Because I have a pension
they cut my benefits in half
Out of that they garnish
my ex's spousal support
If I do any work
they cut my benefits altogether
I am broke

in debt
underwater
& about to lose our home
You call that income?
Outside the high window
Detroit is bone cold
so we sit in his small office
as if we were trapped
To him this is entirely routine
You had a severance? he asks
Yes & I tell him the figure
And where did That go?

It was the thing he did with his mouth
after he asked that question
That was when I decided
to fire him

Out of silence

My friend once took a vow of silence
a whole week in the Smoky Mountains
surrounded by the rustling sunlit trees
birdsong scored at intervals
rain paradiddling on the leaves
little gulps in the puddles
& that fifth night when the wind rose
& the dark thundered with percussion
things falling, turning over
trees creaking as they clung
My friend my poor friend
with nothing but books
prayers & meditation
silent meals silent walks
& silently after the storm
he crept to the one phone booth
on the vast estate & there he sought
not conversation not company
not even chatter
He wanted a human voice so badly
he cracked the white pages

ran a finger down the list
& like Olivier began to recite
the glorious alphabetical names
savoring them as if they were food
& he were starving
thrilling as they left
the empty chamber of his mouth
& made their passage into whisper
It must have been like that
when god broke his silence
& named the animals

Missing

My oldest friend & I in our backyard
one sunny summer. Me sipping ice tea.
He removing his watch & wallet
to sit on a patio chair, relaxing
He palms his thinning wave back.
Fellow seminarians. I ask him about death.
He says & gestures gracefully with his hands,
Look, the dandelions come back every year.
"Those are different flowers, Jim," I say.
His mind hadn't quite left him.
But I watched it in denial.
Watched my friend's body disappear
starting with his memories (like me),
names, words, until he ended up
saying, "Fill in the blanks."
I didn't really become alarmed
until the last time I drove with him.
He would talk & swerve into the next lane.
I drove us then.
Such a sweet judgmental man.
I loved having dinner out

with him until he couldn't read the menus,
or remember what he liked to eat.
And how I tried to help him
when he no longer grasped
the intricacies of a fingerprint ID.
Here's the thing.
I don't want this to be a sad poem
just because I am sad about it.
Even when he lost my name
he still knew I played guitar.
He loved me.
Well, he loved everyone.
His memory warms me.
He was a beautiful beautiful man.
There was no one like him. No one.
In another poem which I can't write now
you'll see him shining with promise,
a charming handsome blonde boy
plucked from the suburbs
with a wavy shock of hair.
You'll applaud his passion for justice,
his real faith in people,
his deep deep courtesy,
his explosive laugh.
He accepted everyone where they were.
I have rarely seen in my 71 years
that.
Fill in the blanks.

Apples

The customers who reek of pee & marijuana
The ones who lie to me
or flirt to try to get a better deal
then ask to see my manager when they don't
The insecure who must be told
which is the most popular color: Black or White
The hurried who look only at my hands
The children who touch everything until it works
The people so needing to trust someone
they trust me
The priests who come out of uniform on
    Saturdays
flockless for a day thank god
The woman who continuously pokes me in the
    side
when she resents the attention I am sharing
They surround me all day with their urgencies
    & moods
their impatience & their gratitude
& they usually leave smiling
like the widow who wanted to return

three items that her husband had purchased
but never got a chance to use
I weigh each item in my hand
return husband widow
& after I check with my manager
& after I deliver the bad news that
unfortunately these items
are not in stock anymore
& thus cannot be returned
she accepts this with a shrug
It was more about making the effort
doing a task her husband would have handled
moving on more than anything
So after we've concluded that business
I ask how she is doing
& she tells me
then offers a hug
& we cry
(I'm sorry but there is no right way to put this
    in a poem)
See every day something like that happens
usually when I am not tired of standing
my feet don't hurt
& I am not nagging a loose tooth in my soul
I feel as if I've come suddenly awake
in a field of black-eyed susans
blossoms hanging their heads in exhaustion

doing a fan dance with their petals
or craning their dark eyes above the crowd
desperately searching
the florescence for any sign of sun
& I have to tell you
there are few days
when I cannot help
falling in love

The Big Thing at The End

The one time I ever fainted
she said
I was furious when they woke me
We laughed that laugh
when you want to hold someone
& say Yes I know yes Yes it's awful
& it may not get better
but we laughed instead
& someone said my friend
was dying from an overdose of penicillin
& he felt nothing but ecstasy
& another said yes
my friend felt the same
when she was drowning
on a perfect summer day
& someone asked what possible
evolutionary purpose
could such a reprieve serve?
Couldn't it all be random?
But it nagged us nonetheless
that in our final passage

we might go gently
& I noticed no one dared
to tender the possibility of
a merciful manager of
survival dispensing relief
though that is what some of us
actually believe or hope
& then our friend whose mother
had survived the camps said
Perhaps it's not for us
but for the predator
rewarding his catch
by pacifying his prey
(who after all is caught)
hastening the transition
from creature to meal
This seemed so shocking
& apt it silenced us
on this lovely evening when
we huddled around
our civilized fire
of coffee cheese & crackers
telling stories of precipices
reassuring the tribe
with tales of great escapes
thrilling chases & close calls
which if one is honest

form the spine of all story
& I believe each of us
became aware
for the briefest moment
of that larger thing
hovering outside
in the brutal winter
& the darker dark
who occasionally listened in
on our little group
of story makers
sometimes observing
our lively heads chatting
in the golden windows
of the night
& thought
Let them talk
Let them talk their heads off

The Last Run of the Pun Trolley

Who among us can resist
the charms of the Pun Trolley?
There is the familiar old
clacka clacka dip dip
of the wheels the dated
turn of the century decor
The back & forth sway
we all assume as we clatter
up the hill or down
& there is that truly
blissful moment
when we reach the turntable
& exit the trolley
& briefly enter the real world
to rotate our vehicle
in a new direction
But it is really only
a return to the start
for the route of the Pun Trolley
is designed to go nowhere
We take our seats

& once again embrace the
clacka clacka dip dip
clacka clacka dip dip
which—can I be honest—
in any other setting
would be considered sexual
But this is the Pun Trolley
Puns have no sexual organs
Puns are jokes without punch lines
Graffiti without the balls to finish
Advertising with nothing to sell
They are ubiquitous as kudzu
but as vulnerable as frost
as soon we'll see

Because today
vengeance has come
to the Pun Trolley
Take a last listen to the
clacka clacka dip dip
Take a good look
at the faux gold bunting
& the buttoned-down
red leather seats
This is the end of the line
There is a stranger onboard
A man in a trench coat

A man who learned the hard way
the secret of the pun
who has patiently repeatedly
unwrapped the fourteen levels of tissue
to arrive at that one little turd
at the bottom of the box
He doesn't say "That's awful!"
or "What terrible taste!"
Or even "You just wasted 10 seconds of my life!"
He knows the punster
needs no validation
Rejection or praise
is beside the point
The point is attention
They hold the public hostage
until they meet their demands
& then they don't release them
Don't you see?
Puns are the violence
the unfunny do
when they realize
they are not funny
They spend all their lives
poking their little puns
into the ribs of a society
too polite to call them
what they are:
Verbal Terrorists

Well today it ends
It ends right here right now
on the last run of the Pun Trolley
I rise & step into the middle of the aisle
I say: May I please have your attention?
Someone says: As long as I can have it back!
Someone else says: Ten Hut!
Someone else says: Quonset hut!
Someone else says: Attila The Hut!
Someone else says: I tilla the soil!
I do not return their smiles
I open my trench coat to unveil
the two rows of dynamite
& the ticking clock
Oh you should see their faces
As far as I am concerned
This moment could last forever

But then like distant drums I hear
clacka clacka dip dip
clacka clacka dip dip
seeps back into my fevered brain
& takes me over once again
takes me to a softer place
Its gentle rhythm soothes
the pulse of vengeance
& somehow something
in me yields & I see

I see I am not surrounded
by the faces of my victims
I am looking in a mirror
Terrorists?
Did I really call them terrorists?
This harmless horde
of word tourists?
If they are evil then
everyone is evil
& nobody can be saved
I breathe & swallow this
hard knowledge
I see their childish pleading faces
I see I am not justice
& they are not sin
God have mercy on my soul!
Who I ask myself is the terrorist here?
Who?
Who has the dynamite?
Who has the timer?
Who has this touchy red trigger?
Whoops

& they wonder where religion came from

Our adopted mother
has gone & left us
It hardly matters why
She could be off
saving a world of strays
feeding the hungry
bringing just desserts
to the peckish
or dispensing treats
to some other
less worthy cats
whom we hate & hope
ice gathers on their paws
For all we know
Mother is never coming back
All we do know
is we have been left
in the so called "care"
of the stinky noisy big man
who frightens us at every turn

In our worst moments
we have no doubts
he killed her
For there she was
and now she's not
It is logic
Didn't he once
kick the black one
off the bed
where mother slept?
Well didn't he?
Didn't he once
lock the golden one in
when he plainly
had business in the night?
Well didn't he?
While he has not yet
stopped feeding us
we have no great faith
this arrangement will continue
So we abase ourselves
We allow his ugly hands
to have their ways with us
& yes we have resorted
to animal sacrifice
If we deliver that which
we ourselves most crave

to the stinky noisy big man
perhaps he will be merciful
& give us what we want in return
Who can fault such logic?
Our first offering:
One Dead Mole
We lay it neatly before
his Lazy Boy throne
It disappears & he does not thank us
The next day we lay another
this one with an instructional
bite out of the rump
should he need prompting
Now it too is gone
The black one saw him
throw it high
across the back fence
toward the creek
We surmise he is teaching
the mole to fly
like those pesky birds
who rarely let us catch them
& mock us daily from
their high perches
Obviously
he is a creature of depth
This stinky noisy big man

who killed our mother
This monster we must
abase ourselves before
Evidently his ways
tower above ours
as the thundering sky
looks down upon the trees
as the trees
dwarf the birds
& as we prey
upon the moles
We have so much
to learn about
the rank of things
Perhaps he will teach us
more if we make
yet another sacrifice
tomorrow

The Boat

I am in a boat.
No. We are in a boat
& it's not a boat
but you know what I mean.

& the boat is going somewhere
Or maybe nowhere.
But it is floating for now.
Unless it's sinking.

It is so comforting to be in a boat.
to have a vessel. A destination.
We don't know the destination.
But at least we're floating.

But then there is the ocean
or this small part of its depth
that surrounds us, buoys us
as if it wanted us to be here get there.

We do not think about the depths.
Below us. The cold dark water:
unbreathable, undrinkable.
Who would want to drink an ocean even if they
    could?

So this boat. This water.
You & I
between here & there.
Is somebody rowing?

In this whole world
there is only you & me & this boat
on this ocean & what happens
depends on us or the ocean.

I say we have to be very careful.
We are only so strong.
A boat is a delicate thing.
& I have never seen an ocean broken.

I say we love each other.
But that is so easy to say.
That means knowing
who we're rowing with.

We did not choose the ocean.
We did not choose the boat.
We did not choose each other.
But we must choose.

—*after September 11, 2001*

The Body Remembers

One night I lost myself in a film about a boy,
cursed with a face only a mother could love.
The planes of his skull were ill–fitted,
a broken vase shabbily repaired.
And he lived with it. Through many bouts
of reconstructive surgery where his features
were rearranged, rebroken & set right
his skin splayed open to reveal
the original mistake, then folded back
like reused Christmas wrapping.
It was a battered thing, his face,
shy & sweet & haunted by
the caring violence it required.
But everybody loved him:
his father, nurses, surgeons, anesthesiologists.
& his gurney was surrounded by toys,
well–known & huggable,
& as he was wheeled to surgery
he smiled at their gentle jokes & touches,
until they had to put him on the table.

Then he wailed & kicked & punched
with a natural terror so obvious
& correct & unexpected, I felt as if
some part of my living skin had been
wrenched away & something inside shaken loose.
And I began to weep & shiver. My body had
    something
to do: it rattled & sparked like a rusty muffler,
a terrifying fit that seemed to come from nowhere.
This went on.
& sometime after I collected the wrung pieces
& rearranged them into something resembling me,
I saw another boy, who on his fifth Christmas
was taken to the hospital before he could open
his gifts, fevered, bleeding from the mouth,
body aching in every imaginable way,
woken every four hours
for needles in the rump, thighs, arms,
so that eventually it became impossible to lie
comfortably except upon his belly.
That was Trench Mouth.
& somewhere in the middle of that ordeal
he had promised God
he would never tell another lie. It seemed
a reasonable vow. Perhaps not logical:
what had truth to do with pain?
But it did the trick. He got better.

From that day on he never told a lie.
He told lots of truths. Awkward truths, stupid truths,
cruel truths, logical truths, righteous truths,
inconvenient truths, harmful truths.
As long as he told truths he was safe.
But he never told of the broken thing that squirmed
within & waited & shaped his life so quietly
he never had a hint it was alive. For 36 years.
He did not know it was there until it was released
& then he did not know how he had contained it.
Surely something that ferocious would need
something bigger than him to hold it in,
something flexible as balloon, something forgiving,
as water reassembles itself when it has been broken,
something warm to calm it, something muscled to
    hold it still,
something grown & intricate: a maze of many
    passages
that could distract it until the boy was safe enough
to face what he had felt.
Nothing is lost. The body remembers.

Obviously I love you but if I were a bird

Yes, obviously, I love you
But, honestly, if I were a bird
I would have the whole sky.
I could touch down anywhere
& every day would be an adventure.
True, I would miss much.
But if I were a bird I would have
no need of walking, hands or doors.
I would take my meals anywhere,
drink from puddles, outfly any
predator, sleep in the treetops,
sing every morning at the top of my lungs.
True, I would leave behind much.
Your face on the pillow next to me.
Your hand enfolded in mine.
Your harmony blending with my voice.
Your laugh, your eyes, your smell.
The way your art gently takes my legs
out from under me & leaves me falling.
Your good sense which grounds me.

Your anger even, which is, admittedly,
a storm to seek shelter from, though
the shelter of your heart is truly
as sturdy as any branch, cozy
as any nest & not incidentally
wider than the sky.

Patrick O'Leary's first novel, *Door Number Three*, was lauded by *Publishers Weekly* as a best book of the year. His second book, *The Gift*, was a finalist for both the World Fantasy Award and the Mythopoeic Award. O'Leary's *The Impossible Bird* was selected as one of *Locus*'s top novels of the year, as was his latest novel, *51*, from Tachyon Publications. He has also published two acclaimed short story collections: *Other Voices, Other Doors* and *The Black Heart*. O'Leary lives near Detroit.

ACKNOWLEDGEMENTS

"The Boat" first appeared in *SCIFICTION.COM* (911 Tribute Online), 2001 and *The New York Review of Science Fiction*, 2001.

"The Body Remembers" first appeared in *Other Voices, Other Doors*, Fairwood Press, 2001.

"Necessary Night" first appeared *The Little Magazine*, Vol. 14, #3 1984.

"I knew" first appeared in *Poetry East* #28, Fall 1989.

"Theology" first appeared in *The Little Magazine*, Vol.14 #4.

"Keep Looking" first appeared in *Jenny*, Spring 2011.

"FUNK" first appeared in *The Little Magazine*, Vol. 14, #3, 1984.

THE NOVELETTE SERIES
from Fairwood Press:

After the Tide
by Jessie Kwak
small paperback: $9.00
ISBN: 978-1-958880-11-1

Hellhounds
by David Sandner & Jacob Weisman
small paperback: $9.00
ISBN: 978-1-958880-02-9

Mingus Fingers
by David Sandner & Jacob Weisman
small paperback: $8.00
ISBN: 978-1-933846-87-3

The Archronology of Love
by Caroline M. Yoachim
small paperback: $6.00
ISBN: 978-1-933846-96-5

The Specific Gravity of Grief
by Jay Lake
small paperback: $8.99
ISBN: 978-1-933846-57-6

Welcome to Hell
by Tom Piccirilli
small paperback: $8.00
ISBN: 978-1-933846-83-5

If Dragon's Mass Eve Be Cold and Clear
by Ken Scholes
small paperback: $8.99
ISBN: 978-1-933846-86-6

Slightly Ruby
by Patrick Swenson
small paperback: $8.00
ISBN: 978-1-933846-64-4

www.ingramcontent.com/pod-product-compliance
Lightning Source LLC
Chambersburg PA
CBHW030235180626
46810CB00008B/3147